# Baseball Saved Us

Written by **Ken Mochizuki**

Illustrated by **Dom Lee**

LEE & LOW BOOKS Inc. • *New York*

*To the Issei and Nisei: American pioneers,
heroes and role models* — K.M.

*For Brian, Eun, Keunhee and all children
who love baseball* — D.L.

Text copyright © 1993 by Ken Mochizuki
Illustrations copyright © 1993 by Dom Lee
All rights reserved. No part of the contents of this
book may be reproduced by any means without
the written permission of the publisher.
LEE & LOW BOOKS Inc., 228 East 45th Street, New York, NY 10017
Printed in Hong Kong by South China Printing Co. (1988) Ltd.
Book Design by Christy Hale
Book Production by Our House
The text is set in Trump Medieval
The illustrations were rendered by applying encaustic beeswax on
paper, then scratching out images, and finally adding oil paint for color.
Some of the illustrations were inspired by photographs taken by Ansel
Adams of the Manzanar internment camp in 1943, from the Library of
Congress collection.

Library of Congress Cataloging-in-Publication Data
Mochizuki, Ken
Baseball Saved Us / by Ken Mochizuki ; illustrated by Dom Lee
p.    cm.
Summary: A Japanese American boy learns to play baseball when he
and his family are forced to live in an internment camp during World
War II, and his ability to play helps him after the war is over.
ISBN 1-880000-19-9 (paperback)
[1. Japanese Americans—Evacuation and relocation, 1942-1945—
Juvenile fiction.   2. Japanese Americans—Evacuation and
relocation, 1942-1945—Fiction.   3. World War, 1939-1945—Fiction.
4. Baseball—Fiction.   5. Prejudices—Fiction.]
I. Lee, Dom, ill.   II. Title.
PZ7.M71284Bas   1993
[Fic]—dc20                                    92-73215   CIP   AC
10  9  8  7  6  5  4  3  2  1
First Edition

## AUTHOR'S NOTE

In 1942, while the United States was at war with Japan, the U.S. Army moved all people of Japanese descent away from the West Coast. They were sent to internment camps in the middle of American deserts up until 1945. The reason, the U.S. government said, was because it could not tell who might be loyal to Japan. None of these immigrants from Japan—or their children, who were American citizens—were ever proven to be dangerous to America during World War II. In 1988, the U.S. government admitted that what it did was wrong.

One day, my dad looked out at the endless desert and decided then and there to build a baseball field.

He said people needed something to do in Camp. We weren't in a camp that was fun, like summer camp. Ours was in the middle of nowhere, and we were behind a barbed-wire fence. Soldiers with guns made sure we stayed there, and the man in the tower saw everything we did, no matter where we were.

As Dad began walking over the dry, cracked dirt, I asked him again why we were here.

"Because," he said, "America is at war with Japan, and the government thinks that Japanese Americans can't be trusted. But it's wrong that we're in here. We're Americans too!" Then he made a mark in the dirt and mumbled something about where the infield bases should be.

Back in school, before Camp, I was shorter and smaller than the rest of the kids. I was always the last to be picked for any team when we played games. Then, a few months ago, it got even worse. The kids started to call me names and nobody talked to me, even though I didn't do anything bad. At the same time the radio kept talking about some place far away called Pearl Harbor.

One day Mom and Dad came to get me out of school. Mom cried a lot because we had to move out of our house real fast, throwing away a lot of our stuff. A bus took us to a place where we had to live in horse stalls. We stayed there for a while until we came here.

This Camp wasn't anything like home. It was so hot in the daytime and so cold at night. Dust storms came and got sand in everything, and nobody could see a thing. We sometimes got caught outside, standing in line to eat or to go to the bathroom. We had to use the bathroom with everybody else, instead of one at a time like at home.

We had to eat with everybody else, too, but my big brother Teddy ate with his own friends. We lived with a lot of people in what were called barracks. The place was small and had no walls. Babies cried at night and kept us up.

Back home, the older people were always busy working. But now, all they did was stand or sit around. Once Dad asked Teddy to get him a cup of water.

"Get it yourself," Teddy said.

"What did you say?" Dad snapped back.

The older men stood up and pointed at Teddy. "How dare you talk to your father like that!" one of them shouted.

Teddy got up, kicked the crate he was sitting on, and walked away. I had never heard Teddy talk to Dad that way before.

That's when Dad knew we needed baseball. We got shovels and started digging up the sagebrush in a big empty space near our barracks. The man in the tower watched us the whole time. Pretty soon, other grown-ups and their kids started to help.

We didn't have anything we needed for baseball, but the grown-ups were pretty smart. They funnelled water from irrigation ditches to flood what would become our baseball field. The water packed down the dust and made it hard. There weren't any trees, but they found wood to build the bleachers. Bats, balls and gloves arrived in cloth sacks from friends back home. My mom and other moms took the covers off mattresses and used them to make uniforms. They looked almost like the real thing.

I tried to play, but I wasn't that good. Dad said I just had to try harder. But I did know that playing baseball here was a little easier than back home. Most of the time, the kids were the same size as me.

All the time I practiced, the man in the tower watched. He probably saw the other kids giving me a bad time and thought that I was no good. So I tried to be better because he was looking.

Soon, there were baseball games all the time. Grown-ups played and us kids did, too. I played second base because my team said that was the easiest. Whenever I was at bat, the infield of the other team started joking around and moved in real close. The catcher behind me and the crowd for the other team would say, "Easy out." I usually grounded out. Sometimes I got a single.

Then came one of our last games of the year to decide on the championship. It was the bottom of the ninth inning and the other team was winning, 3 to 2. One of our guys was on second and there were two outs.

Two pitches, and I swung both times and missed. I could tell that our guy on second was begging me to at least get a base hit so somebody better could come up to bat. The crowd was getting loud. "You can do it!" "Strike out!" "No hitter, no hitter!"

I glanced at the guardhouse behind the left field foul line and saw the man in the tower, leaning on the rail with the blinding sun glinting off his sunglasses. He was always watching, always staring. It suddenly made me mad.

I gripped the bat harder and took a couple of practice swings. I was gonna hit the ball past the guardhouse even if it killed me. Everyone got quiet and the pitcher threw.

I stepped into my swing and pulled the bat around hard. I'd never heard a crack like that before. The ball went even farther than I expected.

Against the hot desert sun, I could see the ball high in the air as I ran to first base. The ball went over the head of the left fielder.

I dashed around the bases, knowing for sure that I would get tagged out. But I didn't care, running as fast as I could to home plate. I didn't even realize that I had crossed it.

Before I knew it, I was up in the air on the shoulders of my teammates. I looked up at the tower and the man, with a grin on his face, gave me the thumbs-up sign.

But it wasn't as if everything were fixed. Things were bad again when we got home from Camp after the war. Nobody talked to us on the street, and nobody talked to me at school, either. Most of my friends from Camp didn't come back here. I had to eat lunch by myself.

Then baseball season came. I was the smallest guy again, but playing baseball in Camp had made me a lot better. The other guys saw that I was a pretty good player. They started calling me "Shorty," but they smiled when they said it.

By the time the first game came around, I felt almost like part of the team. Everyone was laughing and horsing around on the bus. But as soon as we got out there, it hit me: nobody on my team or the other team, or even anybody in the crowd looked like me.

When we walked out onto the field, my hands were shaking. It felt like all these mean eyes were staring at me, wanting me to make mistakes. I dropped the ball that was thrown to me, and I heard people in the crowd yelling "Jap." I hadn't heard that word since before I went to Camp—it meant that they hated me.

My team came up to bat and I was up next. I looked down. I thought maybe I should pretend to be sick so I wouldn't have to finish the game. But I knew that would make things even worse, because I would get picked on at school for being a chicken. And they would use the bad word, too.

Then it was my turn at bat. The crowd was screaming. "The Jap's no good!" "Easy out!" I heard laughing. I swung twice and missed. The crowd roared each time I missed, drowning out my teammates, who were saying, "C'mon, Shorty, you can do it!" I stepped back to catch my breath.

When I stepped back up to the plate, I looked at the pitcher. The sun glinted off his glasses as he stood on the mound, like the guard in the tower. We stared at each other. Then I blocked out the noise around me and got set. The pitcher wound up and threw.

I swung and felt that solid whack again.
And I could see that little ball in the air
against the blue sky and puffy white clouds.
It looked like it was going over the fence.